KT-162-033

EGMONT
We bring stories to life

This edition published in Great Britain 2010 by Dean,
an imprint of Egmont UK Limited
239 Kensington High Street, London W8 6SA
All Rights Reserved

 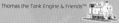

HiT entertainment

ISBN 978 0 6035 6413 0
5 7 9 10 8 6 4
Printed in Malaysia

Edward and
the Brass Band

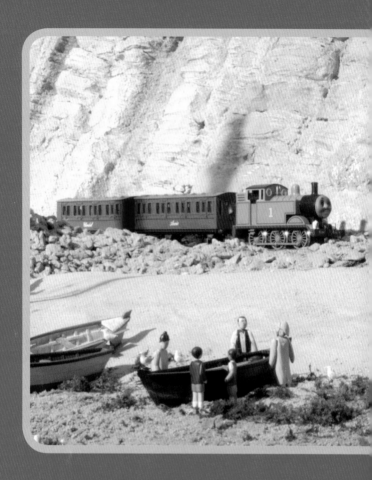

It was Summer on the Island of Sodor and Thomas was happily puffing to the Beach. He was excited to be bringing passengers to the seaside.

He was even more excited because
The Fat Controller was holding his
annual concert at the Castle the
following evening.

Every year, it was Edward's job to take the Brass Band to the Castle for the concert. He was happily humming to himself as he chuffed along the track.

"Pom, pom, pom!" Edward sang.
This was a very important job
and Edward loved being a
Really Useful Engine.

Edward passed Thomas as
he pulled into Wellsworth Station.
"Why are you so jolly today?"
asked Thomas.

"I'm on my way to pick up the Brass Band," Edward puffed, as he sped past Thomas.

Edward could not wait to hear the Brass Band play their wonderful music. He chuffed happily on his way from Wellsworth to Brendam Docks.

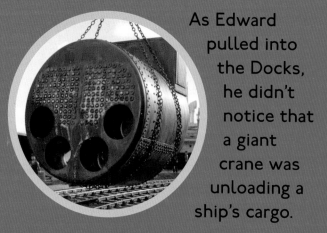

As Edward pulled into the Docks, he didn't notice that a giant crane was unloading a ship's cargo.

It was unloading a huge ship's boiler. The crane swung around and accidentally knocked a horrified Edward right off the track!

"Flatten my funnel!" Edward cried.

One of his wheels had been broken and a coupling rod was bent.

The Fat Controller arrived to find
a very sad looking Edward lying by
the side of the tracks.

"We will get you to the Fitters
Yard straightaway," he said.
"Bertie will have to take the Brass
Band to their hotel."

The fitters worked hard through the night to fix Edward, as a raging storm rolled in from the sea.

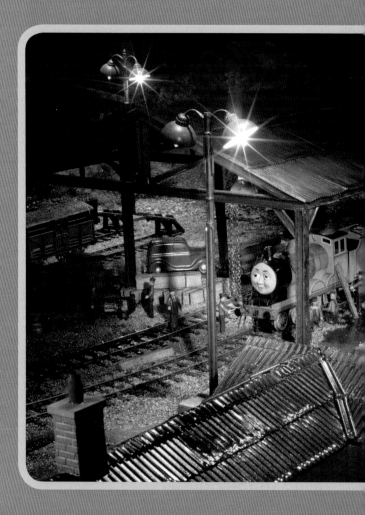

Edward felt even worse as cold rain pelted down and wind whipped around his boiler.

The next morning, the storm
had passed and the sun was
shining brightly again.

The Fat Controller came to see
Edward, but he still wasn't fixed.
"Please, Sir," pleaded Edward.
"The fitters will be finished soon."

"I'm sorry, Edward, the Brass Band can't wait," said The Fat Controller. "Bertie will have to take them to the Castle Concert instead."

"Yes, Sir," Edward replied sadly. He wished he could take the Brass Band.

Bertie set off with the Brass
Band. He was bumping cheerfully
along the country roads, when
he rounded a corner and spotted
trouble ahead. The storm had
flooded the road!

Bertie's Driver decided to take
a shortcut, but it was very muddy.
Bertie's wheels did not like the
mud. They scooted and skated.
They slipped, they slid and then
they sank!

"Oh, no! I'm STUCK!" Bertie cried.

The Brass Band got out and stood at the side of the track, their instruments still in their cases. They were worried they would be late for the Concert. "Tune up your tubas!" the trumpet player cried. "We'll call for help!"

Meanwhile, back at the Yard,
Edward had been fixed and cleaned.
Finally, he was hooked up to his
coaches again.

Edward looked much happier,
but suddenly he heard a strange
noise. "That sounds like Brass Band
music," said his Driver.

"That's not music," wheeshed Edward. "That's a Brass Band alarm!" And, with that, Edward chuffed out of the Fitters Yard and raced to the rescue!

The Brass Band were delighted
to see their old friend, Edward,
when he pulled up beside them.

"I'll get you to the Concert on time!"
Edward cried.

Bertie was very relieved. Edward
had saved the day!

The musicians all climbed aboard, and Edward puffed quickly towards the Castle. They were soon chuffing into Castle Station. The Band said goodbye and thanked Edward for saving the Concert.

That night, the Concert was a great
success. The Brass Band's music
could be heard all over the Island.
Everyone had a wonderful time
- especially Edward!